MY FRIEND GRANDPA

Harriet Ziefert

PAINTINGS BY Robert Wurzburg

Published in the United States 2004 by

Blue Apple Books

515 Valley Street, Maplewood, N.J. 07040

www.blueapplebooks.com

Distributed in the U.S. by Chronicle Books

Printed in China

ISBN: 1-59354-063-9

First Edition

1 3 5 7 9 10 8 6 4 2

MY FRIEND GRANDPA

HARRIET ZIEFERT

PAINTINGS BY ROBERT WURZBURG

Blue Apple Books

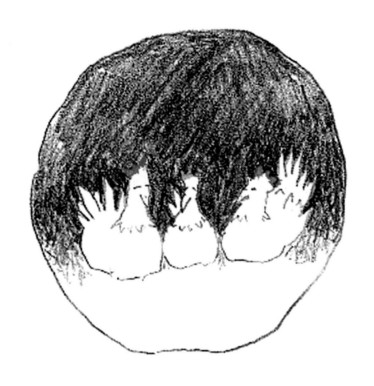

For Isaac Godlin, my friend grandpa
—H.M.Z.

Dedicated to my parents
—R.W.

I'm Emma.
Every summer I spend one month
in the country with my grandpa.

When I'm in the city,
my best friends are Dan, Sarah, and Stella.

But when I'm in the country my best friends
are Grandpa and the big tree that lives on his farm.

There are no kids around who are my age, but I don't mind. Grandpa keeps me busy, and so does his big old tree.

Birds argue. I listen.
Squirrels play. I watch.
Bugs crawl. I collect.

When I want to be high up,

I SWING!

Or I climb.
Yesterday I wanted to see what lives
inside the big hole in the tree trunk.
But I didn't get far.

Pretty soon I found out that up is easy,
but down is very hard.
"Grandpa! Grandpa!" I called, and
he came with a ladder to rescue me.

This morning I woke up early because of a summer storm.

I heard loud thunder, then lightning flashed.

CRACK!

Then came an awful sound.
I looked out across the yard.
"My tree! My tree!
It's been hit!"

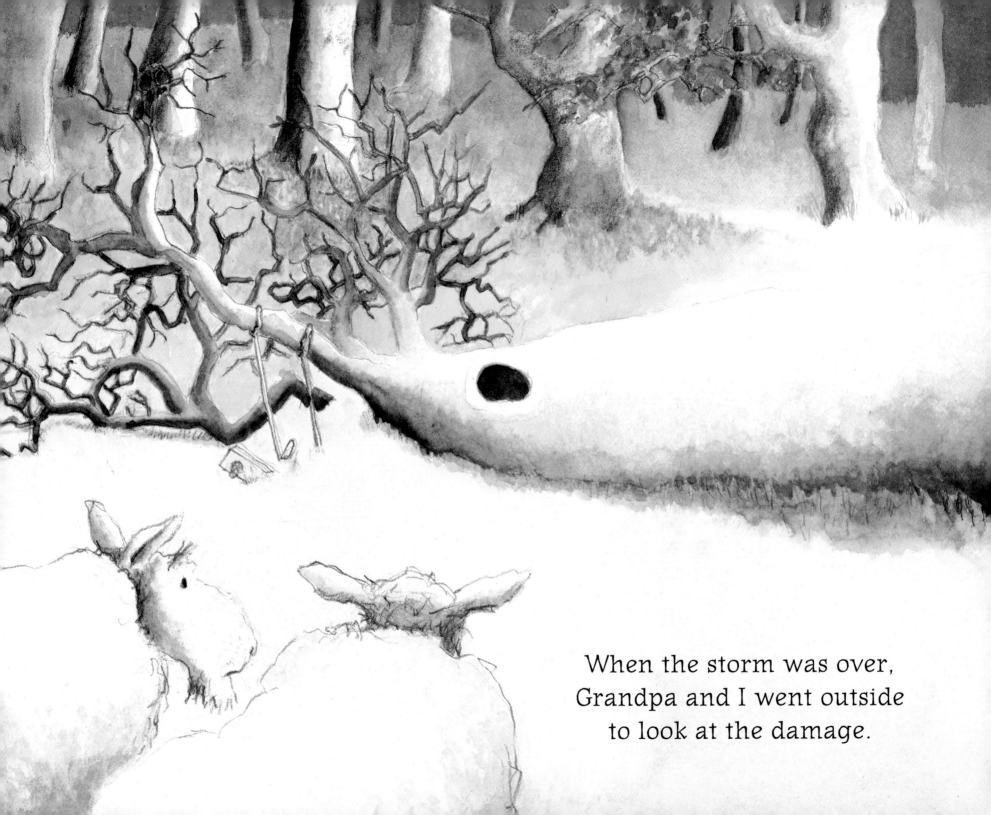

When the storm was over,
Grandpa and I went outside
to look at the damage.

"I'm so sorry, Emma," he said.
"I will have to haul away your favorite tree."

"Grandpa," I begged, "can you save
a part of the tree so it can still
be my friend when I come to visit?"

"I will try," said Grandpa.

Grandpa went to work.
First he used his chain saw.
It was noisy!

Then he started the tractor
and slowly dragged the
tree to a better spot.

I helped Grandpa take away small branches.

Grandpa said they would make good firewood.

Grandpa looked into the hole in the trunk.

He tried to climb in, but he didn't fit. Silly Grandpa!

Then it was my turn.
Grandpa gave me a little push
and I was inside.

Look at me!

We all fit—even Sammy.

Later Grandpa and I sat down to rest.
"It's been a long day, and we're both tired," said Grandpa.
"Let's have an early supper outside and go to bed."

I couldn't sleep.
I wanted to see my tree at night.
"Sammy, come look with me," I said.

I climbed in.
So did Sammy.
Inside was cozy.

An owl hooted. I listened.
A raccoon walked by. I watched.

Then I heard Grandpa whispering,
"It's time for you to be in your own bed."

Good night, Emma.
Good night, tree.